© 2023 All rights reserved. No part of this publication may be reproduced, scanned distributed, or transmitted in any form or by any means, including photocopying, recording, or other electronic or mechanical methods, without the prior written permission of the publisher, except in the case of brief quotations embodied in critical reviews and certain other noncommercial uses permitted by copyright law. Thank you for buying an authorized edition of this book and for complying with copyright laws.

Manufactured in the United States

Any resemblance to actual events or persons, living or dead, is entirely coincidental. This is in no form meant for harm nor do we promote harm. Personal perspective use only. Please do not copy/mimic any words or illustration from this book.

Illustrations by Cameron Wilson for Soulsimplicity Design and Publishing.

21/4/00

DADDY'S SPOILED BRATS

BY 901_NAZCAR
COVER ART BY INDIA N. ANDERSON
BOOK ILLUSTRATIONS BY CAMERON WILSON

Dedicated to my daughters through my storm they never left my side.

The sun is out in Memphis, Tennessee and it would be the perfect day to create fun **_memories_**. "I will be paying the girls an unexpected visit today during dismissal," said Nazcar. While on the way to surprise the girls, he thought of fun activities they might enjoy. It took no time for Nazcar to reach his destination. Nazcar arrived to pick up Brooklynn and Londynn and all he could see were smiling and joyful little faces. The girls ran to the car and jumped in.

"**_Safety_** first," Nazcar told his daughters. Londynn and Brooklynn buckled into their seatbelts, and they were off to YaYa's house for the weekend. While on the way to YaYa's house, Brooklynn and Londynn began to argue over what radio station to listen to. To give them both an opportunity to listen to their music, Nazcar decided to let each girl choose a radio station. The girls could listen to any radio station for 15 minutes each. When the girls were younger, Nazcar created a game with his daughters just for car rides. He would play a few old-school R&B songs and have the girls memorize the songs.

Nazcar, Londynn, and Brooklynn finally arrived at YaYa's house. The first thing the girls wanted to do was to jump on the trampoline. They headed to the backyard where the flipping and jumping sessions began. Brooklynn and Londynn both wanted their dad to watch them showing off their special flips and tricks at the same time. "Daddy, watch me, watch me!" the girls shouted. Taking in the moment, Nazcar smiled and said, "I see you my spoiled brats." Nazcar was excited to see the happiness on his girls' faces. They jumped and played for hours, had snacks, and enjoyed some juice.

Yaya cooked the girls' favorites...wings and fries. While eating, Londynn asked, "Dad are we still going to the Jump World of Memphis?" Nazcar responded, "Yes, you are daddy's little **_princesses_**. Now let's eat up so that we can head out."

After they were done, both girls darted to the car. "I got here first. I made it first." The girls were arguing about who would sit in the front seat with their dad. As a father, Nazcar didn't let anyone sit in the front seat. Nazcar buckled Londynn and Brooklynn into their booster seats in the backseat. He watched the both of them <u>**pout**</u> the entire ride to the Jump World of Memphis through the rearview mirror.

While on the way to Jump World of Memphis, the family passed by The Bike Life Boys of Memphis. The Bike Life Boys are known for popping willies and performing other tricks on their 4-wheelers to get all the kids hyped up.

Shortly after, Nazcar and the girls arrived at Jump World. The girls **_bolted_** off to have fun while Nazcar sat and watched from a safe distance. Two hours later, the girls ran up to their dad bouncing with excitement. "Daddy, we had so much fun today! We love you! Can we do something fun like this next week?" Nazcar replied, "Sure, you spoiled brats."

Brooklynn and Londynn certainly enjoyed their surprise visit today and all the fun things they did together as a family. From jumping to climbing to flipping and most of all, eating the mysterious cotton candy.

It was almost closing time. Nazcar gave the girls a 10-minute warning before it was time to go. On the way home, the girls fell asleep. Nazcar replayed his day with his girls in his mind. Nazcar smiled and thought to himself fatherhood is fun.

SIGHT WORDS

1. **Bolted**- To move suddenly.

2. **Memories**- The mental capacity or faculty of retaining and reviving facts, events impressions ect, or of recalling or recognizing previous experiences.

3. **Pout**- To thrust out the lips.

4. **Safety**- The condition of being protected from or unlikely to cause danger, risk or injury.

5. **Princesses**- Girls who sweet, kind, smart, goofy, intelligent, and beautiful.

www.ingramcontent.com/pod-product-compliance
Lightning Source LLC
Jackson TN
JSHW042008190525
JK14090300001B/1